The Cheeky Monkey

First published in 2000 by
Franklin Watts
338 Euston Road
London
NW1 3BH

Franklin Watts Australia
Level 17 / 207 Kent Street
Sydney
NSW 2000

A CIP catalogue record for this book is available
from the British Library.

ISBN 978 0 7496 3830 6

Series Editor: Louise John
Series Advisor: Dr Barrie Wade
Series Designer: Jason Anscomb

Printed in China

Franklin Watts is a division of
Hachette Children's Books
an Hachette UK company.
www.hachette.co.uk

The Cheeky
Monkey

by Anne Cassidy

Illustrated by Lisa Smith

W
FRANKLIN WATTS
LONDON•SYDNEY

Wendy woke up late
one day.

She walked into the
garden and found ...

... a monkey sitting in
her treehouse.

"Monkey, get out of my treehouse!" Wendy shouted.

"No, I'm staying here!"
the monkey shouted back.

Wendy turned purple
with anger.

"Oh no, you're not!"
she shouted.

Wendy made a plan.

She went into battle with
the monkey.

But the monkey had custard pies.

"Take that!" he shouted
as he threw them at Wendy.

Wendy needed a new plan.

She went to have a look
in her toy box.

Wendy became a pirate.

She was going to capture
the treehouse.

The monkey became a
pirate, too.

He shot at Wendy with
hundreds of peanuts.

21

So Wendy became
a cowgirl.

She made a plan to
capture the monkey.

But the monkey had a better plan and Wendy got very wet.

The monkey laughed and
laughed.

Wendy made another plan.

She went into the kitchen.

Wendy made a trap for the monkey.

He came straight down
from the treehouse ...

... and got straight into Wendy's bed!

Leapfrog has been specially designed to fit the requirements of the Literacy Framework. It offers real books for beginner readers by top authors and illustrators.

The Bossy Cockerel
ISBN 978 0 7496 9141 7

The Little Star
ISBN 978 0 7496 3833 7

Selfish Sophie
ISBN 978 0 7496 9144 8

Recycled!
ISBN 978 0 7496 4388 1

Pippa and Poppa
ISBN 978 0 7496 9140 0

Jack's Party
ISBN 978 0 7496 4389 8

The Best Snowman
ISBN 978 0 7496 9143 1

Mary and the Fairy
ISBN 978 0 7496 9142 4

The Crying Princess
ISBN 978 0 7496 4632 5

Jasper and Jess
ISBN 978 0 7496 4081 1

The Lazy Scarecrow
ISBN 978 0 7496 4082 8

The Naughty Puppy
ISBN 978 0 7496 9145 5

Big Bad Blob
ISBN 978 0 7496 7796 1

Cara's Breakfast
ISBN 978 0 7496 7797 8

Why Not?
ISBN 978 0 7496 7798 5

Croc's Tooth
ISBN 978 0 7496 7799 2

The Magic Word
ISBN 978 0 7496 7800 5

Tim's Tent
ISBN 978 0 7496 7801 2

Sticky Vickie
ISBN 978 0 7496 7986 6

Handyman Doug
ISBN 978 0 7496 7987 3

Billy and the Wizard
ISBN 978 0 7496 7985 9

Sam's Spots
ISBN 978 0 7496 7984 2

Bill's Baggy Trousers
ISBN 978 0 7496 3829 0

Bill's Bouncy Shoes
ISBN 978 0 7496 7990 3

Bill's Scary Backpack
ISBN 978 0 7496 9458 6*
ISBN 978 0 7496 9468 5

Little Joe's Big Race
ISBN 978 0 7496 3832 0

Little Joe's Balloon Race
ISBN 978 0 7496 7989 7

Little Joe's Boat Race
ISBN 978 0 7496 9457 9*
ISBN 978 0 7496 9467 8

Felix on the Move
ISBN 978 0 7496 4387 4

Felix and the Kitten
ISBN 978 0 7496 7988 0

Felix Takes the Blame
ISBN 978 0 7496 9456 2*
ISBN 978 0 7496 9466 1

The Cheeky Monkey
ISBN 978 0 7496 3830 6

Cheeky Monkey on Holiday
ISBN 978 0 7496 7991 0

Cheeky Monkey's Treasure Hunt
ISBN 978 0 7496 9455 5*
ISBN 978 0 7496 9465 4

FAIRY TALES
Cinderella
ISBN 978 0 7496 4228 0

The Three Little Pigs
ISBN 978 0 7496 4227 3

Jack and the Beanstalk
ISBN 978 0 7496 4229 7

The Three Billy Goats Gruff
ISBN 978 0 7496 4226 6

Goldilocks and the Three Bears
ISBN 978 0 7496 4225 9

Little Red Riding Hood
ISBN 978 0 7496 4224 2

Rapunzel
ISBN 978 0 7496 6159 5

Snow White
ISBN 978 0 7496 6161 8

The Emperor's New Clothes
ISBN 978 0 7496 6163 2

The Pied Piper of Hamelin
ISBN 978 0 7496 6164 9

Hansel and Gretel
ISBN 978 0 7496 6162 5

The Sleeping Beauty
ISBN 978 0 7496 6160 1

Rumpelstiltskin
ISBN 978 0 7496 6165 6

The Ugly Duckling
ISBN 978 0 7496 6166 3

Puss in Boots
ISBN 978 0 7496 6167 0

The Frog Prince
ISBN 978 0 7496 6168 7

The Princess and the Pea
ISBN 978 0 7496 6169 4

Dick Whittington
ISBN 978 0 7496 6170 0

The Elves and the Shoemaker
ISBN 978 0 7496 6581 4

The Little Match Girl
ISBN 978 0 7496 6582 1

The Little Mermaid
ISBN 978 0 7496 6583 8

The Little Red Hen
ISBN 978 0 7496 6585 2

The Nightingale
ISBN 978 0 7496 6586 9

Thumbelina
ISBN 978 0 7496 6587 6

The Magic Porridge Pot
ISBN 978 0 7496 8611 6

The Enormous Turnip
ISBN 978 0 7496 8612 3

Chicken Licken
ISBN 978 0 7496 8613 0

The Three Wishes
ISBN 978 0 7496 8614 7

The Big Pancake
ISBN 978 0 7496 8615 4

The Gingerbread Man
ISBN 978 0 7496 8616 1

* hardback

Rhyming stories are available with Leapfrog Rhyme Time